# My Family
## Jasper the Cub

Author: Gill Bennet
Illustrator: Terry Georgiou



ISBN: 9798475672150

ACKNOWLEDGMENTS

Avril Clark, Cameron Bennet, Christina Blossom Berman,
Maria Worsfold, Steve Berman

Jasper the baby lion is the youngest cub in his family.

His older brother and sister always liked playing together.

Jasper tried so hard to fit in with his family. But no matter what he did, he always felt like he was different.

When learning how to hunt for food, Jasper just couldn't get it right.

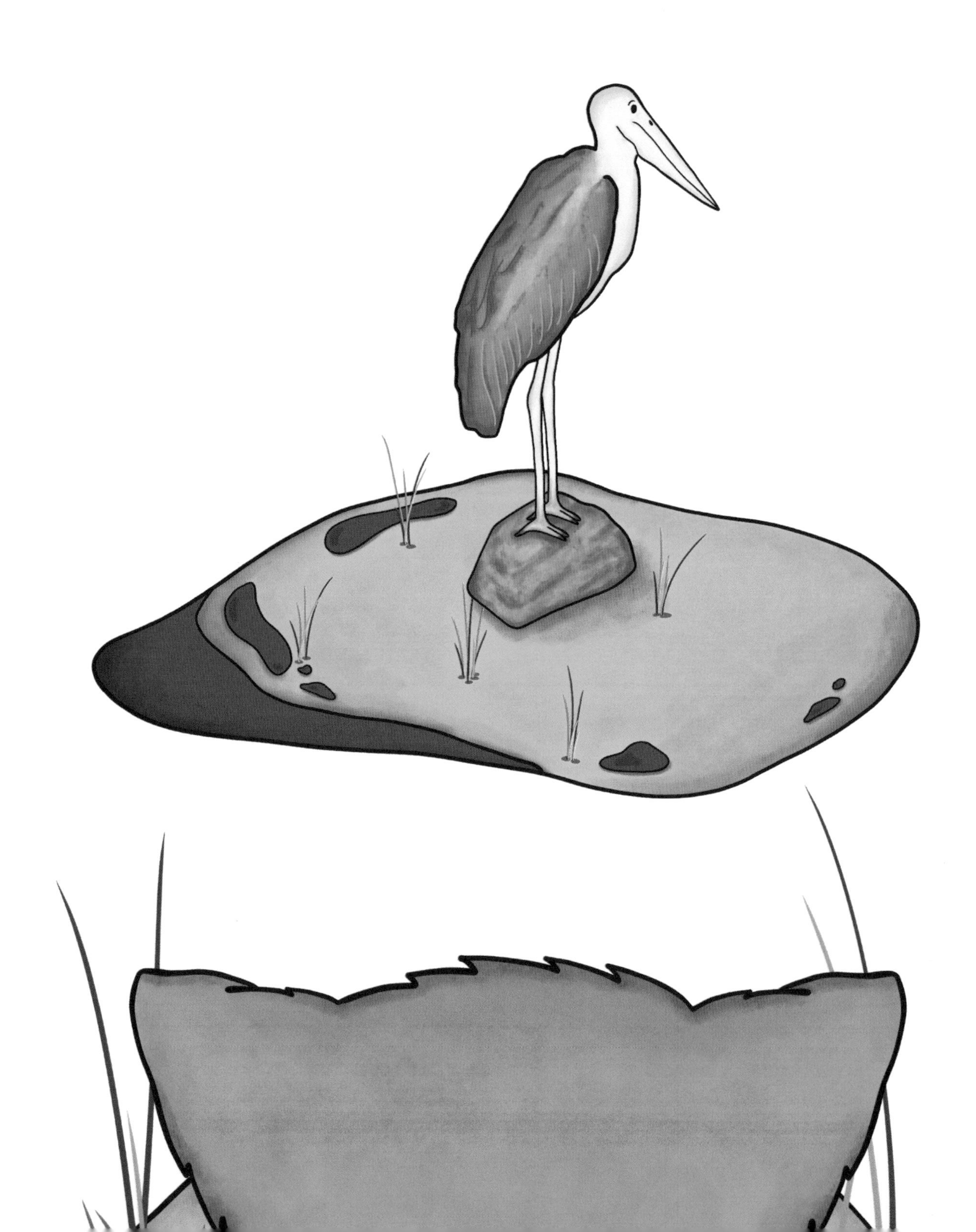

His brother and sister would laugh at him. Jasper started to think that he wasn't a very good cub.

Even though he tried his very best to be like the rest of his family, Jasper felt like he didn't belong.

One day down by the stream, Jasper met a new animal.

I'm Jasper and I'm a cub. I live with my family. We keep each other clean and work together when hunting for food.

My name is Albert and I'm a tortoise. I have a big shell on my back that I use as my home.

I'm glad I don't have to hunt for food, I can just nibble on some fresh grass when I am hungry.

Jasper became sad.

I'm not very good at hunting. I wonder if I was ever meant to be a cub?

I understand
what you mean.

I love being a tortoise but sometimes I do wish I could be a turtle. I wish I could swim with my cousins in the ocean. That would be great!

Suddenly… Jasper had a great idea!

What if we trade places? I think I would like to be a tortoise rather than a cub.

Albert thought
about it for a
moment.

OK! Learning to be a cub sounds like fun! I have
never thought of being anything else except a
tortoise. But I would love to give it a try.

Over the next few days, Jasper taught Albert how to be a cub and Albert taught Jasper how to be a tortoise.

First, Let's hunt for bugs.
Get ready to jump and catch the bugs, Albert.

Ready...**steady**...

**GO!**

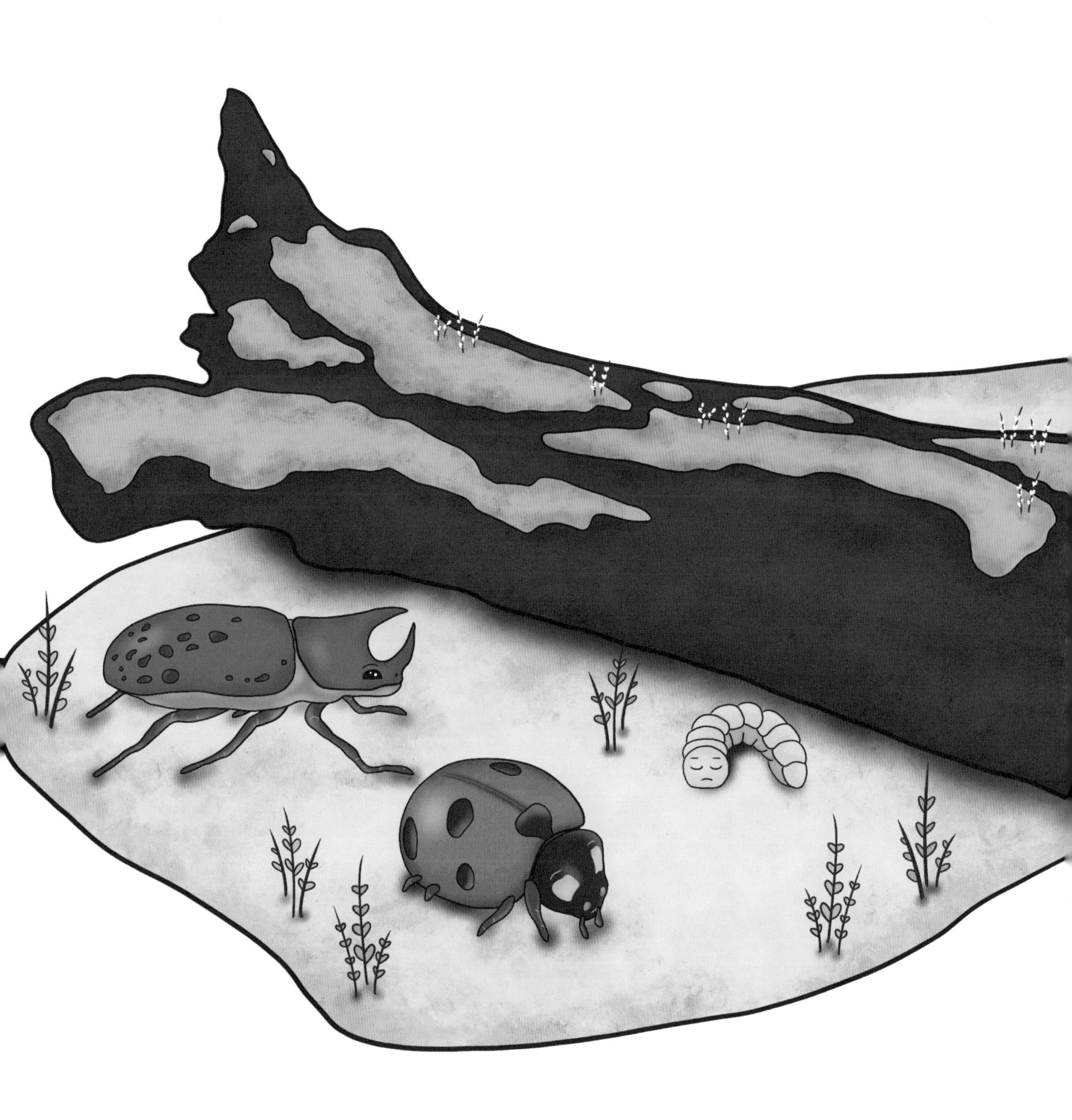

Yes! We got some! You have done so well Albert.

That was so much fun! Thank you, Jasper.

Next, Jasper taught Albert
how to roar like a lion.

ROAR
ROAR
ROAR

Then it was Albert's turn to show Jasper how to be a tortoise.

Here Jasper, I found you a tortoise shell to wear on your head.

It’s a perfect fit!

Thank you
Albert for my
tortoise shell.
I love it.

The next day Albert taught Jasper how to dig a hole to keep cool from the hot sun.

I feel so much better
Albert. I'm beginning to
feel like myself.

Albert took Jasper to surf on the ocean waves,
with his tortoise shell.

Look how high we are Albert! This is the best day ever!

One day, Jasper was walking along, with his tortoise shell on his head. Suddenly, his brother and sister turned up with tortoise shells on their heads too.

Jasper quickly turned around
and looked at Albert surprised.

I told your brother and
sister you're happier
being a tortoise and don't
want to be a cub
anymore.

Jasper was worried.

I love being a tortoise. I hope they don't want me to go back to being a cub.

Don't worry, they just didn't understand so they decided to try it themselves to see why it made you so happy.

Jasper beamed with joy.

Jasper ran over to Albert and gave him a big hug.

Then Jasper and Albert walked over to the rest of the cubs and joined in with their fun.

Jasper was very happy because now he knew that it didn't matter if he was a cub or a tortoise, his brother and sister loved him no matter who or what he wanted to be.

See you all on the
next adventure

Eliza the Goldfish

Book coming soon

Printed in Great Britain
by Amazon